EMERALDS FOR ENVY

BY

R J KALPANA

THE BEJEWELLED FAMILY SAGA

BOOK - 4

Emeralds For Envy (Fiction/Novel)
Copyright © R. J. Kalpana Ph.D 2020

First Published - May 2020

Published by –Pen & Ink Solutions, Chennai - 600090
Contact: penandinksolutions@gmail.com

This novel is a work of fiction. Any resemblance to actual persons, living or dead is purely coincidental.

All rights reserved. No part of this publication may be reproduced, stored in or introduced into a retrieval system or transmitted in any form or by any means (electrical, mechanical, photocopying, recording or otherwise) without the prior permission of the publisher. Any person who does any unauthorised act in relation to this publication may be liable to criminal prosecution and civil claims for damages.

Cover Image - Victorian painting, Anonymous.

EMERALDS FOR ENVY

Who first beholds the light of day

In springs sweet flower of May

And wears an emerald all her life

Shall be a loved and a loving wife

- Harriet Bishop

R. J. KALPANA

*The fabled eastern gems of the Bejewelled
One, the Queen's
jewels are more cherished than gold and more
valued than life itself. It is said that only the
worthiest may behold them for they are promised
riches and happiness beyond dreams.*

EPISTLE

Yours most exalted Person, His Grace, Duke of Andover,

Salutations, your Grace! I pray this missive of mine finds you safe.

I have received your message. I was happy to note that you were able to convince the misguided young lady to select another *nom de plume*. For in these perilous times, it is most prudent to use names that are tried and tested by the English public.

May the young lady be blessed with joy in her choice of protector and may she be safe!

A trifling matter was brought to my attention last evening, your Grace, for a woman well past her first bloom was taken into Newgate Prison. She was raising Cain to such an extent that she brought attention to herself by such means.

The Warden was firm in his opinion that she stole some bread apparently for her young child and yet, stealing is an offence as you are well aware, your

Grace.

The woman was once upon a time in a most respectable position. She was working, I believe, as a nurse for a well-known noble family. But now, unfortunately, she seemed to have fallen into hard times as is evident by her attempt to steal something as paltry as bread without any finesse whatsoever that is usually to be found amongst such people.

I most humbly beg your Grace's condescension to kindly free her from the horrors of Newgate. I swear by my mother's grave that you won't be disappointed.

I remain yours most humble and obedient servant,

Timms

PROLOGUE

The sound of screaming and death cries below started penetrating the walls of the castle. The children huddled together wondering what was happening. Soon they will know. Soon they will make a decision that will change their lives forever. Soon they will part forever.

The nursery door flung open and their elder brother, Dominic, ran into the room with a sword in his hand. He skidded to a stop in front of them and took a moment to look at them.

"My beloved sisters and brothers" Dominic said tearfully. "The Graces, the Duke and Duchess, mama and papa…" his voice broke but he swallowed the tears and continued manfully, "They are dead and the Rajah's men are coming after us now."

There were screams and tears all around him until he lifted his hand and silence once again filled the room as his brothers and sisters looked on with bravely but with tears coursing down their cheeks.

"We will fight them," said Wulfric. His second

brother as he stepped forward with fists clenched. Mr. Timms protested.

Dominic once again lifted his hand and stopped the flow of words as his sisters and brothers all agreed to fight.

"The fight will be for another day. This I promise you. Mama and Papa's death will not go avenged. We will not rest until the land is stained with the Rajah's blood."

They all nodded solemnly.

"But today we are not prepared. Today we must part ways and hide. It will confuse the Rajah and his men for they will not know where to find us. As long as we are alive, even one of us, we will avenge their deaths."

"Will they come for us?" asked Sita crying.

"Yes they will. We have the Queen's Jewels. The Rajah covets them and he must have them at any cost. Remember the story mama and papa told us about how papa helped mama escape from India..."

"And they fell in love and mama stayed on in England," finished Leila.

"Yes but the Queen's Jewels are mama's heritage and the Rajah sought to steal from her."

"We will not give it to them," tumbled the determined words around him.

"No! We will not!" agreed Dominic. "But for now, go and be safe. Stay alive! At any cost!"

They promised they will stay alive at any cost clutching the Queen's Jewels in their childish palms.

They gathered the nursemaids and footmen and told them exactly what must be done. Timms instructed them where to go and whom to meet and how soon to contact.

Then Dominic took over. He solemnly kissed each of his brother and sister and pressed their own gems into their hands and made them and their guards swear to keep them safe.

"I will come for you," he promised solemnly. "Then we will be together again. One family."

With this promise ringing in their ears, the children parted ways and escaped from the castle Andover through its secret passages known only to the family.

They ran confident that their elder brother will come for them and that they only have to hang on long enough for him to make everything safe for them to be together once again.

CHAPTER ONE

It was the darkest hour before dawn. The fog curled and uncurled its way throughout London, at times unveiling palatial mansions and grim hovels and quickly veiling them from human eyes.

The chilling cold of the fog seeped into the jacket of Adrian, Duke of Winterbourne as he watched with half-hooded eyes out of the window at the street.

The candle flame sputtered and died out leaving a burnt smell lingering in the air. The Duke flared his nostrils at the smell and leaned slightly out of the window to inhale the cold night air.

He wondered wearily if it would be better to retire for the rest of the Season to his country seat, Chateau de Winter but then he doubted if life would be any different there either. He was tired and weary of the same pattern repeating in his life over and over again.

A shadow moved at the far right and Adrian

turned his head idly to gaze at what caught his attention so briefly. Nothing stirred for one infinite moment but slowly one shadow detached itself from the rest and began to move stealthily hugging the wall.

He held himself still as he followed the shadow as it made its way towards him. It stopped short at the drawing room window when the shadow arched upwards and grasped the window sill to haul itself up.

One hand lifted to push at the window which opened gracefully and silently. A testimony to the diligence of the Duke's staff who oiled the doors and windows regularly so neither would be so presumptuous as to creak.

With great indolence Adrian leaned against the window sill and watched with detached interest as the shadow disappeared through the window into his drawing room. He wondered vaguely what the thief would find worthy to steal in the blue drawing room.

The paintings were too heavy to carry and anyways the more important paintings were hung in the picture gallery at the Chateau and not here in his London townhouse.

Perhaps the Dresden figurines his mother collected and which lay artfully scattered across the mantelpiece of the great fireplace and around the room he mused. Minutes passed and then slowly but surely the door to his study swung open softly.

A sudden surge of anticipation thrummed through his veins as he watched from his position in the shadows the thief creep into the room. The sound of a match and a muted flame flickered forth from the candle on his desk. His breath held as his eyes beheld the most exquisite beauty standing rifling through his desk.

As much of a beauty as could be perceived through all that grime and dirt he thought. She looked up and slowly swung her head round calculating the room and all its contents in the dim light of the candle.

He wondered what it was she was searching for and if perhaps he could be of assistance. He nearly grinned at that thought. The only assistance he was willing to provide was to have her in his bed assisting her out of her clothes and dirty ones at that.

She had now moved on to the paintings tried to move them around to look for hidden cache. He then decided he had enough of this and moved out of the shadows of the window curtains.

"May I be of assistance my lady?" he drawled.

She nearly dropped the candle in her terror as she swung violently around. His breath stilled as he caught her eyes in the candlelight liquid caramel and now wide-eyed with fear.

"Who are you?" she asked anger taking over and masking her fear.

"Duke of Winterbourne at your service, ma'am," he said and bowed elegantly although his cravat was undone.

"Why are you hiding in your own home?" she asked belligerently almost as if she blamed him for her theft gone bad.

"Well, pardon me," drawled the Duke sardonically "I am flattered by your attention to what a Duke must do in his own home."

She turned crimson at that. He looked at her with interest as he noted the flush a faint pink start at the base of her neck travel up until her whole face was red.

"My, that's an interesting way to blush," he noted with interest. "Never seen anything quite like it before."

Which made her flush even more and her fingers tightened on the candleholder.

"Must be difficult in your profession," he mused. "Such a dead giveaway don't you think?" he asked tilting his head at an angle as he sought to peruse her like a bird would before it pounced on the worm.

"I don't know what you are talking about, your Grace," she said imperiously as she slowly edged her way to the door.

He watched with interest her crablike manoeuvre.

"It is ill-manners to leave in the middle of a

conversation you know," he said conversationally.

"Oh, is that what we were engaged in your Grace?" She asked almost sweetly that had his dander up immediately.

"No?" he asked curiously. "What would you call it then?"

"Casting aspersions and calling me names, your Rudeness," she replied tartly.

She was almost at the door and another moment she could dash through it and out the window and the house.

"My-my, that's quite an accusation," he countered. "I was merely stating facts, my dear."

"I am not your dear," she replied indignantly as she slowly let her hand drift towards the handle of the door.

"Would you like to be?" he asked intrigued.

"What?" she squeaked.

Suddenly, she noticed that he was much closer than before. He was looming over her like a great big shadow darker and for the first time she felt a little fear. Her heart jolted at the nearness of him where she could smell bergamot and sandalwood and the fresh air and perhaps her fear as well.

She stared up at him and for the first time she noticed how handsome he was in the classical sense. An aristocratic nose which probably looked down upon lesser mortals with hauteur she thought angrily when she noted his nostrils flaring a little in disgust probably at her smell. God, even she knew she reeked of St. Giles and the rookery but there was nothing she could do about it. She lifted up her chin pugnaciously as if to provoke him to do his worst.

As he looked down at her, she noted a little resentfully that he had the most beautiful eyes she had even seen. They were green, glittering like emeralds that her mama used to tell her. And then just like that the tears flooded her eyes.

Adrian looked down at his little thief, trying so hard to be brave and failing miserably. God, she reeked like a midden heap. He sighed. But then she had the most exotic eyes tilting at the corners and they were caramel lush and good lord - flooded with tears.

"Come now *mignonne* there is nothing to fear," he said as he stepped closer to her prepared to stop her escape if necessary.

"I am not crying," she replied angrily dashing a hand at her eyes. "I never cry."

"Yes, of course," he agreed gravely. "I can see that."

"Now, if you are quite done questioning me, your Lordship," she began defiantly.

"You have a more important engagement?" he asked curiously.

"None of your business, your Nosiness," she lifted her nose haughtily in the air in return.

"Well, leave if you must," he said and stepped back, bored.

CHAPTER TWO

She threw him a startled glance and wearily with her eyes still on him, she opened the door to his study and darted into the hallway. He noticed she went back into the blue drawing room and he leisurely strolled to the window sill and waited. After a few moments, a shadow silently slid out of the drawing room window and tumbled onto the garden floor.

He laughed silently, waiting and watching for what else she would do. As she crept silently away, another shadow detached itself from the wall and hurled itself upon her. She cried out in a startled voice and tried to regain her balance.

Adrian flung his long legs over the window and dropped to the ground on the other side and stood silently waiting for the event to unfold itself. The light from the street identified the second shadow as a swarthy coarse young man who held onto the little thief and gave her a shake, "Did you get it?"

"Let me go," she cried even as she fruitlessly

tried to escape from his hold.

"I knew you were good-for-nothing," snarled the coarse young man and gave her a slap that even Adrian could hear.

His Grace of Winterbourne strode forward and gripped the assailant's wrists and bore them downwards with merciless strength that belied by his foppish appearance. His victim gave a whimper of pain and sank quivering to his knees.

"Milord! She is the thief, milord. I am merely seeking to correct her behaviour," he begged.

His Grace bent over the young man standing a little to one side so that the light of a nearby street lamp fell on that white agonised countenance.

"Surely she is a little young and ahh...untrained for this game?" drawled the Duke. "Or did you take me for a fool?"

The young man flushed and sneered, "I was seeking to protect you, milord," he begged. "If she sought to rob you, milord, she shall pay for it! Ungrateful brat! I will make her sorry, milord, I promise you! A thousand apologies milord!"

The Duke released him and raised a scented handkerchief to his aristocratic nostrils. "Keep your distance, my good man. No doubt beating is good for the young."

The girl shrank closer to him. "That's not true, your Grace. I..."

"Shut your mouth gel," the young man said

angrily standing up and dusting his behind. "Milord has better things to do than listen to you."

"Who is she?"

"My sister, milord. I have cared for her since our parents have died and this is how she repays me, with ingratitude."

"No!" she said her eyes flashing in anger. "He is not my brother."

"Shut up," the young man said and raised his hand threateningly.

"I will buy her," said his Grace calmly.

The young man stared uncomprehendingly.

"Milord?"

"I suppose she is for sale," his Grace mused to himself.

"I am not for sale," said an indignant voice beside him.

"She is a good 'un milord. A hundred pounds would do nicely."

She gasped.

"I will give you a guinea."

"No milord! She is worth much more!"

"Then keep her," said Winterbourne as he turned to leave.

The girl ran to him, clinging to his arm. "Your Grace! Please take me. I will work for you. I swear!"

His Grace paused. "I wonder if I am a fool?" He lifted up his hand and gazed at his long, slender aristocratic fingers and then he sighed and removed a ring from his small finger. A diamond winked and sparkled in the light of the lamp.

"Well, fellow, will this suffice?"

The man gazed at the jewel as though he could hardly believe his eyes. He rubbed his eyes and drew nearer.

"The girl is yours, milord," he said and stretched his hand greedily.

Winterbourne tossed the ring at him and turned and returned back to the house. At the last moment, he turned and walked across the garden to the great front door and knocked.

His butler opened the door surprised to find his master standing on the doorstep when he thought he retired for the night.

"I know Gibbons it is a bore trust me," said his Grace as he languidly stepped into the house and walked towards the study.

Bowing lackeys sprang to open the double doors admitting him, looking in surprise at the shabby figure who came in his wake.

He walked to the fireplace where a lackey was busy lighting a fire and stood quietly watching the shrinking child by the door.

"Well, what have we here? A whim? Come here child."

The girl came to him timidly.

"Cat got your tongue? God knows you had a

lot to say a while earlier." His Grace commented silkily.

The girl blushed and shook her head.

"Quite a pretty child. Now, what am I to do with you?"

Her stomach growled at the moment and her face went up in flames.

Winterbourne laughed, "Well, that answered my question. I suppose I ought to feed you. Now, be a dear and ring that bell over there."

The girl went obediently and rang the bell. Gibbons almost immediately appeared at the door.

"Ah Gibbons, always so efficient. Bring a tray of food here," instructed the Duke.

The girl looked at him shyly, "Please milord, I can wait if you please."

"I do not please child. Go, sit down and eat."

He sat down as he spoke and lifted up his hand once again to gaze at his fingers now missing one diamond ring.

After a moment's hesitation, the girl turned and went to seat herself at a small table by the door throwing quizzical glances at him once in a while. Gibbons soon brought up a tray of cold cuts and a large glass of milk.

The Duke gazed out of the window and drummed his fingers on the desk. He had no idea why he bought the child and what he is going to do with her. *Maman* would not be pleased if she would ever come to know.

And yet, there was something about that child, some subtle hint of quality. She was of gentle birth. One can tell from her speech, and her delicate hands and face. One only had to look at the way the girl ate her food. Dainty little bites like a debutante. Even with hunger eating up her belly. For another, innocence shined from those caramel eyes.

The girl finished her food for she stood up and pushed back her chair and walked up to him and suddenly knelt at his feet and kissed his hand. "Thank you, your Grace."

Winterbourne disengaged himself but the girl still knelt looking up into his handsome face with humble eyes.

"No need to thank me child. It is obvious you haven't had much to eat."

"I thanked you for saving me from Mickey, my lord," the girl answered softly.

"You are reserved for a worse fate," said the Duke sardonically. "I now own you."

"Yes, your Grace, if you please," murmured the girl and sent him a swift glance of admiration from under long eyelashes.

The thin lips curled a little. "The prospect pleases you?"

"Yes, your Grace. I will serve you faithfully."

"What is your name child?"

"Leonie"

"Now tell me Leonie, what were you doing with this errr....Mickey?" asked the Duke curiously.

"Mickey framed my nurse Anna for stealing, your Grace," she replied angrily. "Anna would never steal. And when they locked up Anna at Newgate prison, Mickey told me that I have to steal from you and with that money, he will free Anna from Prison. He brought me here."

"What were you supposed to steal from me?"

"Jewels," said Leonie shortly.

"Dear me!" said Adrian and gazed pensively into the fire.

After a while, Leonie said softly, "If you please your Grace, I will work tirelessly for you night and day but would you please have Anna released from the prison?"

Adrian looked at her in surprise.

"She is a good person, your Grace" said Leonie passionately. "She looked out for me and worked so hard to pay for my studies and everything. I cannot bear to think of her rotting in prison when I know it's my fault she is there in the first place."

Suddenly Leonie's eyes filled with tears.

"Why would it be your fault?" asked the Duke coldly.

"Because Mickey wanted to sell me to this Madam but Anna said that she was a bad person and that she runs a brothel where gentlemen come and … and…and told me to run and hide whenever

Mickey comes around."

The Duke took in her distressed face and teary eyes and sighed and rang the bell. Gibbons ever prompt answered the summons.

"Take her to the Rose chamber, Gibbons and get her a bath and a nightgown. Present her to me tomorrow after breakfast with a suitable morning gown."

He turned to look down at Leonie still kneeling at his feet. "Rise child and go with the estimable Gibbons. I shall see you tomorrow and we shall talk."

Leonie came to her feet and curtsied gracefully, "Thank you, my lord."

She kissed his hand and turned to leave.

The Duke regally inclined his head and watched Leonie go out behind Gibbons. He sat quietly for a long time while contemplating the darkness outside his window. He puzzled over the events of this evening and thought about the players.

He had long learned the value of trust and loyalty and he knew they were priceless. He understood what bound these players together. Louise wearied him and suffering as he was from ennui he found this to be the perfect form of amusement. No one learnt to curtsy like that in the backstreets of London. Here was a fine mystery for him to solve.

CHAPTER FOUR

Shortly after noon the following day, Winterbourne sent for Leonie who came promptly and curtsied prettily and knelt to kiss the Duke's hand.

Gibbons had obeyed his master's command implicitly and in the place of the grim, shabby, stinking child of the evening before was a scrupulously clean and neat young lady whose chocolate curls were tamed with a white ribbon running through them and whose slim person was clad in a simple muslin gown with a chocolate ribbon tied around her waist.

Winterbourne surveyed her for a moment. She was even more beautiful once she cleaned up.

"Yes, you may rise, Leonie. I am going to ask you some questions. I desire you will answer them truthfully. You understand?"

Leonie nodded shyly sitting herself down on the footstool beside his chair, "Yes, your Grace."

"Now, tell me your name."

Leonie looked at him surprised, "But I said last night, your Grace, my name is Leonie."

"What is your full name child?"

"I don't understand, your Grace," said Leonie puzzled. "I have always been called Leonie."

"Who are your parents?"

"They died, your Grace. I was just the baby you see. Only Anna explained it all to me when I sufficiently grew up."

"What were their names?"

"Mama and papa, I used to call them but I don't know your Grace"

"Where were you born?"

"I don't know, your Grace. Not in London I think for I remember the countryside."

"Where did you learn to speak like a lady?"

"Oh, that was Anna's doing your Grace," said Leonie blithely gesturing with her hand. "She paid the vicar who used to come to the stews for Sunday service to teach me my letters, and to read and write and Latin and Greek and many other things."

Adrian raised his eyebrows. "You got all this education in the stews? Why?"

"I don't know, your Grace. I was the baby, you see and the favourite Anna said."

"Favourite of whom?"

"Everybody's favourite. There were bad people, your Grace that killed my parents Anna said and so we had to run and hide. Anna said that when my big brother, Dominic, will come then everything will be alright and we will be family once again," Leonie nodded.

"Give me your hand."

Leonie extended one slender hand for inspection. Adrian took it in his and surveyed it. It was small, finely made with long tapering fingers slightly roughened with toil.

"Yes" said the Duke. "Quite a pretty hand."

Leonie smiled engagingly.

"You have very beautiful hands your Grace, I think" she said.

The Duke's lips quivered. "You put me to the blush child with your compliments. Now go and rest in your room, I will send for you in the evening."

Leonie stood up slowly, curtsied and said, "Yes your Grace."

She departed closing the door carefully behind her.

The Duke waited awhile and then slowly rose and strolled out calling for his coach. In half-an-hours' time he was seated in his coach heading towards Newgate Prison. The answer to his questions apparently lay with Anna.

He arrived at the Fleet and walked towards the great arched entrance. He nodded to the guard standing outside and walked in straight to the office of the warden of the Fleet. A scarred brute of a fellow dressing down one of his cringing subordinates.

He looked up with a start at the esteemed company and shook himself, "What is it milord?"

"The Duke of Winterbourne, my good man," said Adrian gently. "I am here to see one of your prisoners, Anna, I believe, her name is."

"Well, your Grace, prisoners are not allowed visitors," said the warden sourly.

"Do I look like a visitor to you?" asked the Duke sarcastically and then lifted his hand up and said, "No wait, don't answer that, I don't want to tax your non-existent brain."

"Now see here your Grace," began the warden belligerently.

Winterbourne reached across the table and hooked his fist in the warden's collar and dragged him half-way across the table.

"Now see here my good man, if Anna isn't standing in front of me within the next minute, you will standing in front of your Maker," whispered the Duke very very softly and then turned to the guard.

"Bring Anna here," he commanded.

Within half-a-minute, a tired young woman was standing in front of him.

The Duke looked her from top to toe and asked "You are Anna?"

The woman dropped a curtsy and said, "Yes milord."

"Your charge is one Leonie?"

Anna looked up alarmed.

Winterbourne let the warden go tossing a purse full of coins at him and turned to Anna and said, "Come, Leonie is awaiting you."

He walked away and Anna ran to keep up with him. He gestured to her to enter the coach and entered in after her.

"Your Grace?" Anna began worriedly.

Winterbourne held up a hand to silence her.

"After we have reached home Anna, I have a number of questions for you which you will answer to my satisfaction. And then you may meet Leonie. She has not come to any harm and is now housed as my ward. After rescuing her from the clutches of Mickey, I think I am entitled to some answers."

"Yes your Grace," said Anna tiredly.

They arrived back at Winterbourne residence in a short while and the Duke descended and made straight for his study with Anna running to keep up with him. He went to the sideboard and poured himself a glass of brandy and glanced at Anna and poured a second half-glass and handed it to her. Then he went to sit in an armchair by the window.

"Now, Anna! That you may not misunderstand me or seek to evade me, let me tell you that I am the Duke of Winterbourne. I am said to have a formidable reputation. No man has crossed me and lived to tell the tale. Yes, I thought that might be of shock to you. You do realise, it is dangerous to play games with me. I am going to ask you a few questions about your charge, Leonie and I desire you to speak only the truth."

"Yes your Grace," said Anna clutching the glass tightly.

"Who are Leonie's parents?"

"The Duke and Duchess of Andover, your Grace."

"Good lord. She is one of the missing children?"

"Yes your Grace. The youngest," Anna nodded. "You must have heard how they were murdered in a cowardly manner and to protect the children from the Rajah's men we separated and we ran. I was nurse to little Leonie then."

"And this brother of hers, Dominic?"

"The first born and the heir, your Grace and now, he is the current Duke and I don't know where he is. He promised all of us that he will make things safe and that he will come for us but…I fear for his safety your Grace." Anna looked at him helplessly.

His Grace fell into musing at this fount of information.

"Begging your pardon, your Grace," said Anna after a while shyly. "May I ask your intent towards Lady Leonie, your Grace?"

The Duke turned and looked at the tired woman standing in front of him reeking of St. Giles and the prison, clutching her glass with whitened dirty fingers and yet, with hope and worry clashing in her eyes, ready to do battle if she must.

"Don't worry Anna," said his Grace gently. "You have done your duty towards your charge. But now, you can leave her safely in mine. It is time she dressed and lived like the daughter of a duke. Her education, though you have done a commendable job still needs completion and I will see to it. Once her education is complete, I will introduce her to my mother who will launch her into Society. You may continue on as her maid."

A smile beamed on Anna's face on hearing this and she dropped into a curtsy, "I thank you, your Grace."

His Grace rang the bell and Gibbons answered the summons.

"Ah, Gibbons, please inform Lady Leonie to attend to me," commanded the Duke.

Gibbons nodded and closed the door.

In a short while, a white whirlwind ran into the room and breathlessly closed the door, "You asked to see me, your Grace?" she asked and then curiously turned to look at the woman standing in front of the Grace.

"Anna?"

The woman turned towards her.

"Anna! My Anna!" Leonie cried and flung herself at Anna sobbing and laughing at once. "Oh,

Anna, you won't believe what happened to me. Mickey said, Mickey did..."

"There, there milady, its all going to be fine. You be forgetting what Mickey said or did," said Anna patting Leonie's head.

"Yes but Mickey made me steal from his Grace only I didn't know how and I was caught but his Grace let me go but Mickey wouldn't. He slapped me Anna but his Grace came and rescued me. And now I am wearing this pretty dress and living in this pretty house," said Leonie breathless after her recitation.

Anna nodded and said, "Come milady, make your curtsy to his Grace. We shouldn't intrude on his time. You can show me your room."

Leonie nodded obediently and dropped a curtsy to his Grace and smiled beautifully at him. "Good day, your Grace."

Then she turned and caught hold of Anna's hand and dragged her out of the room laughing in joy and chattering all the time.

CHAPTER FIVE

The next day Leonie and Anna were bundled into his Grace's travelling coach and taken to Chateau de Winter while the Duke himself rode his favourite stallion beside the coach. Leonie spent the entire journey hanging out of the coach and talking to the Duke. With their arrival began Leonie's education into the fine art of being a lady.

Leonie was enchanted with Chateau de Winter and demanded to know its history. She walked with Adrian in the grounds and learned how one of the Winterbourne ancestors came with William the Conqueror and settled here building the Chateau. Different wings were added by the later generations and its illustrious guests numbered every one of the Kings and Queens of England.

Her education at Adrian's hands was a great source of interest and amusement to her. In the music room, he taught her to dance with an eagle eye for the smallest fault or the least hint of awkwardness in her bearing. But fortunately, Leonie possessed considerable natural grace and took to her lessons like a swan takes to water.

Anna would come and watch indulgently while they trod the stately measure. She did her best with her charge's education but dancing was beyond her abilities. She reflected that at times like these the unapproachable Duke was almost human as he laughed with the little sprite of a girl.

Adrian made her practice her curtsy and taught her to combine her pretty roguishness with some of the haughtiness that characterises a Duke's daughter. He showed her how to extend her hand for a man to kiss, how to use her fan.

He would walk with her in the long corridor of the picture gallery teaching every rule of deportment until she was perfect. He insisted that she cultivate a certain queenliness in her bearing. She applied herself enthusiastically and was radiant when she earned a word of praise from him.

He took her outside and taught her to ride. She rebelled against the side-saddle saying mama always rode astride for Anna said so.

Adrian laughed and said, "You may ride astride brat but there are times in London when you have to ride side-saddle so it is best that you get used to it Leonie."

So they rode together in the grounds until she mastered the art of riding both astride and side-saddle and then they went all over the countryside. But those who saw this beautiful young girl beside the

Duke exchanged knowing glances at each other for there had been other beautiful girls at the Chateau.

The Chateau so long bereft of a proper mistress began to wear a more cheerful air. Leonie's youthful spirit pervaded it as she flung back the heavy curtains and opened windows to let in the sun.

She tumbled the cushions and left her ribbons lying at odd places caring nothing for Anna's shocked protests. Adrian permitted her to do as she pleased. It amused him to watch her blossom with confidence. He liked to hear her give orders to his lackeys. She had an air of command, unusual she might be but never once did she exhibit a lack of breeding.

Her lessons were soon put to test. At times he would say suddenly, "I am the Dowager Duchess of Winterbourne and you have just been presented to me. Show me your curtsy."

"But you cannot be a Duchess, your Grace," Leonie objected. "You don't look like a duchess. You be the Duke."

The Dowager Duchess. Show me the curtsy."

Leonie sank down and down. "Like this right? But not so low as to the Queen. This is a very good curtsy, your Grace."

"It is to be hoped that you don't talk as much," remarked his Grace tartly. "Spread your skirts a little more and hold your fan thus. Show me again."

Leonie obeyed meekly.

"It is very difficult to remember everything. So many rules," she complained. "Let's go riding again, your Grace."

"Presently. Curtsy now to a Countess."

She swept her skirts regally and with head held high extended one small hand. Adrian smiled.

"Curtsy now to me."

Leonie sank down with her head bent and raised his hand to her lips.

"No, my child. That was the curtsy for the King. I am but an ordinary mortal remember."

She rose. "This is the way I like to do it your Grace," She smiled enchantingly. Adrian was hard put to correct her when she was exercising her charm to full effect.

At other times he fenced with her. She enjoyed this most of all. As she one day confided in him saying, "Anna said that mama used to fight with swords and daggers. Will you teach me, your Grace?" She looked up at him artlessly. He was ensnared.

She donned shirt and breeches for this pastime and displayed no little aptitude for the game. She had a quick eye and a supple wrist and she soon mastered the rudiments of this art.

The Duke was one of the finest swordsmen of the day but this in no way discomposed Leonie, so intent was she in learning the skill. He taught her the Italian style of fencing and showed her many subtle passes that he learnt abroad.

She experimented with one of them one day and because his Grace's guard at that moment was lax, she broke through. The button of her foil came to rest right at his heart.

Leonie danced in excitement. "I have killed you your Grace. You are dead."

"You are bloodthirsty," remarked Adrian.

"But it was so clever of me, wasn't it your Grace?" she cried.

He relented and said, "Sure you are."

She learnt to throw her dagger in perfect accuracy. Adrian thought that indeed her mother's blood must be coursing through her veins.

After dinner he always talked to her of the personalities of the day, explaining who they were and their role in Society.

"You will meet them all one day child," he explained one night. "So it is better to be prepared."

Leonie nodded from where she sat on the footstool. And sometimes Adrian would say, "Tell me of your life in St. Giles."

Leonie rested her head against the arm of his chair and gazed dreamily into the fire. The cluster of candles threw a light over her curls that turned the chocolate colour to burnished copper so that they seemed to come alive and on fire in the golden light.

Adrian lightly tousled her curls. She sighed.

Leonie's delicate profile was turned towards the Duke and he watched it inscrutably noting each quiver of the fine lips and each flicker of the dark lashes.

Leonie told him her tale, hesitantly, shyly, glossing over the sordid parts and her voice fluctuating with every changing emotion. Winterbourne listened in silence, sometimes smiling, sometimes sad, and most times angry.

The hardships were evident more by what Leonie didn't reveal rather than by what she did. There was never any complaint or allusion to the cruelties she had to undergo at St. Giles but she always spoke glowingly of Anna.

Leonie put a timid hand on the Duke's sleeve and said, "But then you bought me your Grace and gave me everything. I shall never forget your kindness."

Adrian was moved to protest but Anna came quietly in and paused at the threshold of the Duke's study staring at the two of them by the fire.

"Ah, Anna has come." He flicked Leonie's cheek with one careless finger. "Bed, my child."

CHAPTER SIX

The following morning, his Grace decreed that Leonie's education has come to an end and it was time for her to make her debut in Society. So they packed up once more and drove to London. But this time instead of driving straight to his Grace's residence, they drove over to his mother's home.

Leonie sat nervously in the drawing room with Anna and his Grace, as the butler went up to his mother's chamber to inform her that his son was visiting with guests.

"Do you think she will like me, Anna?" asked Leonie nervously picking at her white muslin gown.

Anna looked at the enchanting figure her charge presented in her muslin gown with ribbons threaded through her shiny curls and privately thought the Dowager Duchess would have to be blind and completely heartless not to be taken in by this lively sprite.

"You will be fine milady," said Anna encouragingly. "Just stop fidgeting."

Within moments, his *maman* flew through the door shrieking.

"Adrian! How delightful to see you. It has been such an age since you visited your *maman*." She would not let him kiss her fingertips but flung her arms about his neck and embraced him.

"I have been positively bored. You would not believe how tedious life has become."

Adrian knew perfectly well how monotonous life could get but instead disengaged himself and smoothed his sleeve.

"I trust I find you well, *maman*?"

"Yes, oh yes! And you Adrian? I vow I have missed you quite dreadfully. Why! Who is this?" Her eyes alighted on Leonie sitting demurely on the sofa.

"This, my dear, is your ward."

Lady Fanny Winterbourne fell back a step and looked at him in surprise. "What is the meaning of this Adrian?"

"Sit down *maman*," said Adrian impatiently. "I will tell you the complete tale."

So Lady Fanny sat down promptly and at the unfolding of the tale, she alternatively cried and laughed and grew angry.

"Oh, you poor child. Come here dear," she beckoned Leonie who went up to her and sank into a curtsy before her.

"Charming and well done but kiss me now and sit beside me," said Lady Fanny pulling her into a hug and kissing her and then patting the seat next to her.

"I used to know your mama dear and I was there at the party that night."

"You knew mama?" gasped Leonie looking up in wonder at Lady Fanny.

"Ah, your parents love was legendary my dear as were their deaths unfortunately," she sighed. "Come, let us not get maudlin. Adrian, I vow you know exactly how to bring me out of my megrims. I would enjoy chaperoning dear Leonie. Why, it will be like having a daughter."

Adrian smiled at the announcement and looked at Leonie. "Well, child, you will stay here from now and I will occasionally call upon you. Be guided by *maman* in everything and you will not go wrong."

Leonie looked up at him and whispered, "Your Grace, please do not leave me."

Lady Fanny overhearing the faint whisper looked up in surprise and cast a questioning glance at Anna who merely tightened her lips in response.

"I shall come and see you very soon *mignonne*. You will be safe here."

"But you don't understand…" her big eyes filled with tears.

"I do understand. Have no fear. I shall come to visit you soon. Perhaps you would like to go for a turn in the Park tomorrow?"

He turned to his mother and bowed. "I have to thank you madam. Tonight, let Leonie rest; tomorrow is soon enough for Society to see her. Farewell."

With that he went out shutting the door behind him.

Left alone with Lady Fanny, Leonie looked helplessly at the closed door wringing her hands.

"Come child, no need for tears. Didn't Adrian promise he will take you for a ride in the Park tomorrow? I will show you to your rooms" said Lady Fanny kindly.

"Yes milady," said Leonie subdued and walked with Lady Fanny up the stairs to her chambers.

She led the girl into her rooms and said, "I vow it will be most entertaining to dress you up. Do think of all the clothes."

She turned to look at Leonie. "Hmmm, these are pretty clothes but you need better ones dear if you have to go about in Society. The first thing to do is call the modiste here."

From then onward, the word spread of Lady Fanny's new ward and Society was curious. The house was bustling with activity what with the dressmakers, the milliners, the dancing masters, the coiffeurs. Every aspect of Leonie was cursorily examined and determined and approved. Soon London began to hum with tales of her beauty.

The next day, Leonie slipped away escaping from dancing masters and dressmakers and stole into the study waiting for the Duke. He arrived that afternoon prepared to take her for a jaunt at the Park and saw her listlessly trailing from window to desk to window.

"Well, *mignonne*?"

She ran to him and sank down on her knees in front of him. "Your Grace, all of this..." she gestured widely, "It frightens me."

He stroked her bright curls caressingly.

"What frightens you *bebe*?"

"All these grand people, grand mansions, grand parties, and everyone is so busy."

"You do not like it?"

She wrinkled her nose cutely and said, "It excites me your Grace but then I remember St. Giles."

"Ah, my dear child, you will strive to forget St. Giles," he admonished her pulling her to her feet. "You are now the ward of the Dowager Duchess of Winterbourne and you have always been her ward. You have never been to St. Giles, you have never heard of St. Giles. Yes?"

She nestled her hand in his and gave a tiny sigh, "Yes, your Grace."

"Come, my child. It is too fine a day to stay cooped indoors."

Her eyes sparkled with pleasure and she ran off to fetch her wrap, bonnet and parasol. She returned almost immediately.

He lifted her up into his curricle, then went round to the driver's seat as his groom climbed to his post in the back. Gathering the reins, he snapped them smartly over the backs of his high-stepping blooded chestnuts.

The horses' clopping hoof beats rebounded off the neat cobbled stones as his curricle rolled down the street. He urged his team into a canter and Leonie laughed delightedly. Her hair flying behind her loosened from her coiffure. He grinned at the rare treat of showing off in front of a beautiful girl.

Hyde Park was crowded with mounted riders and open carriages. Slowly, Leonie noticed the stares they drew. Young men gawked openly at her, while matrons smiled and gracefully inclined their heads. Word spread quickly he knew. Soon everyone knew that he was escorting his mother's ward around Town.

"They are staring, your Grace," said Leonie worriedly as she tried to snuggle into his side.

His Grace bit a smile and gently held Leonie away. "They are admiring your beauty Leonie. Let them."

He pulled up beside a landaulet, tipping his hat he said, "Well met, Lady Jersey. Allow me to introduce you to my mother's ward, Lady Leonie."

Leonie quickly smiled and bowed her head.

Lady Jersey looked at her critically and said, "Yes, Fanny has been telling me about her ward and how much she enjoys having her around, like a daughter. I can see she is beautiful and with pretty manners. But that's to be expected from your mother's ward. Tell Fanny that I will send over the vouchers for Almacks."

"Thank you, my lady. Leonie is charmed."

"Well, I suppose you don't want to keep your horses waiting so go on. I will see you at Lady Hamilton's ball tonight?"

"I believe that is correct my lady. *Maman* has decided that she would like Leonie to be introduced to the Ton tonight."

"I will see you there."

He turned his curricle once out of Hyde Park and he slowly tooled them towards home.

"Well Leonie, how did you like the ride?" he asked casting her a sideways glance.

"I liked it very much, your Grace," she said willingly. "Do you think I can ride my horse here?"

His Grace laughed and said, "Not astride my dear. One of these days we will ride but it won't be soon. If I know my mother, there will be a never ending list of parties you will be attending."

"What if I don't want to your Grace?" asked Leonie quietly.

"What's this?" asked Adrian sharply.

"I think I would like to go back to Chateau de Winter," she said smally.

"All in good time my dear but for now London awaits your presence and we shall make the most of it."

She nodded visibly sad that they had reached home. He set the brake, stepped down from the curricle and went around to assist her while his groom moved to the horses' heads.

He tousled her curls and carelessly said he will see her tonight and drove away without entering the house.

CHAPTER SEVEN

Later that evening, Adrian propped one shoulder against the ballroom wall and sipped meditatively at a glass of champagne as he watched Leonie step into the arms of yet another man.

Leonie glowed in a gossamer gown of soft white brocade. Leonie's feet peeped from beneath the lace petticoats in shoes of white satin with heels that were studded with tiny diamonds. The single white rose with the diamond hair pin that Adrian gifted her nestled in her curls just above her left ear.

Without doubt she was a Toast. Lady Jersey stopped by earlier and remarked, "She is a breath of fresh air, your Grace. She will have the Ton at her pretty feet by the end of tonight."

Adrian noticed she wasn't lacking any invitations for dance. She was laughing at something her partner said for her eyes were sparkling and her lips parted like ripe cherries and her cheeks were faintly flushed.

Something uncomfortable stirred in his heart and he straightened just as the music came to a halt. He lifted up his hand and Leonie ran to him.

"Oh your Grace, isn't this exciting? I have been introduced to everybody and I have been dancing nonstop since" she confessed breathlessly.

Adrian smiled at her artless chatter and said, "Shall we sit quietly awhile do you think?"

"Yes please your Grace. I would like that very much."

His Grace led her through the ballroom onto the balcony and into the gardens below and seated her at a neat little fountain.

"How do you like your first ball Leonie?"

"It is very enjoyable your Grace. I danced with a great many people and they were all so grand but they were all kind to me as well."

"I am glad to hear it child," said his Grace gravely. "If you are too tired, we can retire for the night. You only have to say the word."

"Yes your Grace, but my lady Fanny bade me attend to her after every dance."

"As is proper child. Come, you have had your rest, I will restore you to my lady."

Leonie obediently stood up and walked with him to where all the matrons were seated.

"Adrian," she hailed after seeing her son with her ward. "I have presented Leonie to everybody. I have enjoyed myself prodigiously."

"Thank you *maman,* you have achieved your goal."

"Yes yes; now do go away, Leonie has yet to dance with young Edward, heir to a considerable fortune I heard."

Adrian smiled tightly and bowed and left the ladies.

Later that evening, Leonie stepped out onto the balcony with young Edward. She was beginning to tire and she saw his Grace dancing with a beautiful woman dripping with diamonds.

She turned to young Edward and asked, "Who is the lady his Grace is dancing with my lord?"

Edward looked at the ballroom and said, "Oh, that is Countess Marling."

"His Grace likes her?"

"I was told he loved her once but she married another and is now a widow. It looks like she is angling to become a Duchess."

"Oh!"

"Come, let's not talk about them. Let's talk about us. Will you let me call upon you?"

"I am thirsty my lord, can I get some lemonade please?"

"Of course my lady," said Edward and bowed low and took himself off to the refreshment table.

Leonie saw his Grace holding the Countess close and said something and they both laughed.

She felt a tightening in her chest and so she turned and walked into the gardens. She didn't realise she had wandered off until a hand clamped on her shoulder.

She turned around in fright. "Mickey!"

"Well, well, well, look at you, dressed all pretty," Mickey sneered, bruising her shoulder.

"Let go of me," Leonie said and shoved him.

"Did you get the jewels yet?" he grabbed her hair and pulled.

"Ouch! No, let me go."

Leonie was struggling real hard now.

"I could have got a pretty penny for you," said Mickey angrily. "Now, you have cost me."

"Dammit Mickey, let go!" Leonie kicked him and tried to claw him.

When suddenly his hold loosened and he was pulled away by a very angry Adrian.

"What the hell are you doing here?" asked Adrian ruthlessly strangling Mickey.

"Adrian, your Grace, please let him go," Leonie cried frightened, trying to get Mickey loose.

Adrian flung him away and turned to look at Leonie.

"Come here," he said.

Leonie flung herself at him, clutching his shirt and bursting into tears.

Adrian held her close, his head resting on hers

and he turned to look at Mickey and found he was gone.

He slowly pushed her away and said, "Stay here, I will get your cloak and make your apologies to *maman*. I will tell her you have a headache. Then I am taking you home."

Leonie nodded sniffling.

Adrian came back quickly after giving his mother a message and led her to the back of the garden and through the wicket gate onto the side street. There they waited for his carriage and when it arrived, he lifted her in and sprang inside. The carriage sped away into the darkness.

"What was that all about?" he asked silkily.

Leonie sat in a corner afraid. "I just took a walk in the garden while waiting for Lord Edward to get me a glass of lemonade but I forgot where I was and when I remembered Mickey had already caught me."

"Why?"

"Why your Grace?"

"What did he want with you now?"

"He kept asking me to steal the jewels from you, your Grace. He said he could have made money out of me one way or the other."

"Why did you walk in the gardens, Leonie? You know you are not supposed to do that."

Leonie kept silent at that.

"Tell me."

"I saw you dancing with Countess Marling, your Grace."

"So?"

"You never danced with me! Lord Edward said you loved her but she married someone else and now that she is a widow, she wants to marry you."

Adrian sighed and gazed out of the window at the dark streets occasionally lit up by the street lamp.

"Jealousy doesn't become you child," he said quietly.

"Neither does toying, your Lordship," she replied pertly.

Adrian looked at her surprised and gave a bark of laughter. "I believe I really should beat you for your impertinence."

"I will run away."

"I will find you."

Leonie sniffed pulling at her torn bodice. Adrian saw the gesture and his mouth dried at the picture she presented. He forced himself to look away.

"What is with this obsession with jewels?" he asked exasperated.

"I do not know your Grace," said Leonie candidly. "Mickey is not even a thief."

"No?"

"No. I think he works for that madam at the brothel that Anna told me about. That's why he talks often about selling me to her."

Adrian involuntarily clenched his fists. "He will not get a chance *mignonne*."

They arrived at his mother's house and he wrapped her up in a cloak and carried her inside all the way up to her bedchamber.

He set her down on the carpet and glanced down right into her lush caramel eyes. He could feel her pressed into him. His blood pounded. She was a vision in white silk. He slowly dipped his head and brushed his lips across hers.

She sighed softly and leaned into his kiss. It was his undoing.

"Ahh child, I shouldn't."

"Yes, you should," she whispered. "Please."

"You will meet some young gentleman…"

She nodded pressing herself closer.

"He will court you and marry you."

She kissed him. It was untutored but her lips were soft and gentle and inviting. Adrian moaned her name, and dipped his tongue between her lips unable to resist the soft temptation of her mouth.

The new intimacy shattered whatever control he had been exerting over himself. He slid his hands down her body tracing her curves and her spine and gently pressed her against him, revelling in the softness of her body.

Adrian licked her tingling lips, too innocent to understand his desire was being held in check by a very thin thread. He kissed her once more unable to resist and regretfully pushed her away.

"Your Grace?"

"Ahh love, you are temptation itself," he sighed. "I am a cad to take advantage of your innocence."

"I don't mind," she said shyly peering at him through her eyelashes.

"I suppose tomorrow you will be at home for visitors," he drawled. "I better come and keep an eye on you."

"Yes, your High and Mightiness," she said cheekily.

He cracked a laugh and without looking at her he walked out of the door just as Anna was coming in.

"Ah Anna, your mistress had a slight mishap. Take care of her," said his Grace said as he ran down the stairs.

CHAPTER EIGHT

His Grace was angry. His coachman took one look at him and crossed himself. Somebody was going to die tonight he thought. And when he received his orders from His Grace to go to the grimiest stews, he knew it for a certainty.

The streets were narrow with refuse from the kennels on either side of the road. The houses were tumbledown stacked haphazardly with nary a window between them. The curtains were ragged and dirty and it had rained a while back so that the paving stones were slick with water and refuse. Moonlight gleamed dully on the greasy roads.

The coachman pulled up the coach and as the lackey sprung to open the door, his Grace said, "Find out where the brothel is and where Mickey is right now?"

"Yes your Grace," said the impassive lackey. He stepped up to the loungers and money exchanged hands and words were whispered.

He returned smartly and said, "Your Grace, I

believe Mickey is generally found to be at the local tavern at this time."

"What are you waiting for? Take me there," commanded his Grace coldly.

The tavern of Hammer and Tongs was situated midway down a squalid street and from its open door issued the stench of foul ale and cabbage stew. The coach pulled up in front of it and one of the lackeys jumped down to open the door for his Grace to alight.

His Grace stepped slowly down from the coach, his handkerchief held to his nose. He picked his way across the filth and garbage to the inn door and entered what appeared to be the taproom. The interior was full of smoke and heated by a fire on the hearth.

There was a sullen atmosphere to the place. A handful of patrons were scattered along the long wooden trestle tables. Several of them glanced up in surprise as his Grace walked in. They began to eye him greedily.

For each pair of gutter rat eyes took note of the expensive long rose-lined purple cloak carelessly draped across the shoulders and was allowed to fall gracefully revealing a coat of purple satin heavily laced with gold, a waistcoat of gold flowered silk and a lavish sprinkling of jewels on his cravat and breast. A silk hat perched atop his head with a long beribboned cane in his right hand. Although a light dress sword hung at the side, the hilt of which was lost in the folds of his cloak.

Adrian could almost see the wheels in their collective heads spin. He would welcome the fight if anyone were foolhardy enough to attack him. He glanced around and saw the coarse young man at the rear near the door. Mickey looked like he had downed one too many bottles of gin.

He looked up and gasped when he saw Adrian place his leg on the bench in front of him.

"Hello Mickey," said his Grace suavely.

"I didn't do nothing guv'nor," said Mickey nervously flicking his eyes around.

"Tut-tut-tut," said his Grace gently. "Lying isn't good for the soul. What did I say the last time we met?"

"To leave the gel alone," muttered Mickey sourly.

"And tonight you didn't heed the warning," his Grace sighed loudly. "What am I to do with you?"

"It 'ain't my fault. I am being hounded as it is," said Mickey irritably.

"Hounded by whom?"

"Who knows?"

His Grace slowly opened his coat and pulled out his dagger and started cleaning his nails with it. Mickey gulped at the sight.

"What's with these jewels?"

"I don't know, your Grace. These men, they

come from India and they wants me to steal some emerald from you. I am not a thief, I told them so"

"Yet?"

"Well, she was of no use staying in the stews with her high and mighty ways and that maid of hers not letting anyone comes near her. I had to do something, right?"

"Wrong," said his Grace as he reached over and twisted the Mickey's collar and bodily lifted him up over the table to the other side.

"I gave you fair warning not to go near Lady Leonie and you have chosen to disregard it leaving me with no choice but to carry through. Prepare to meet your Maker Mickey."

"No, your Grace, please. I will not go near her again, I promise," pleaded Mickey terrified.

His Grace lifted the dagger and slit his throat open and flung him aside.

There was pin drop silence as the patrons watched aghast. He turned to face them wiping his dagger on his handkerchief.

"Let this be a warning to all of you. Come near mine again and that will be your fate. Let it be told that I well know how to protect mine."

With that he swept out of the door to his coach.

Across the town in his mother's townhouse, Anna was berating her mistress.

"What were you thinking milady, allowing

his Grace to take such liberties with you? Tearing your clothes off? Never heard the likes of it," scolded Anna as she busily started removing the torn gown from Leonie.

"But Anna, it wasn't his Grace's doing," Leonie protested. "It was Mickey again."

"Never say so milady," said Anna round-eyed with shock.

"I was walking in Lady Hamilton's gardens when Mickey accosted me. When I was struggling with him, he tore my dress and that's when his Grace arrived. He pulled Mickey off of me. He gave his apologies to Lady Fanny and told her I had the headache and then whisked me away in his carriage and brought me here."

Anna sighed as she sat her mistress down in her chemise and began removing the ribbons in her hair. "It is my fault that you are being constantly subjected to such unwanted attentions milady."

"Oh no Anna, how can you say so?" said Leonie turning to look at Anna. "You took such good care of me and worked yourself to the bone to pay for the vicar for my studies."

"Hush child. That's neither here nor there. I should have taken you to the countryside. You might have been safer there."

"But Anna, there wouldn't have been any work in the countryside for us and then I wouldn't have met his Grace," said Leonie sadly.

Anna looked sharply at her charge. "Now, don't you go pining for the moon milady," she warned.

"I know Anna, I know," said Leonie wisely.

Leonie got into her nightgown and was in bed having dismissed Anna, when she heard footsteps in the hallway and the door swung open and Lady Fanny swept in.

"What is this child I heard, you have a headache?" asked Lady Fanny worriedly.

"I will be fine after some rest my lady," said Leonie sitting up in bed.

"La child, it was too much excitement all at once eh?" Lady Fanny nodded her head. "I know the feeling. I felt the very same way at my first ball."

"Did you madam?" asked Leonie politely.

"Of course child, the expectations of it all but never you mind, tomorrow we will take it easy. Why, we will have an at-home tomorrow and perhaps, if you like any of the gentlemen who call upon you then you may take a ride in the Park with them."

Lady Fanny nodded approvingly. "Yes, we will stay quietly at home tomorrow."

"Thank you my lady for taking such good care of me," said Leonie.

"Shush my dear child," waved Lady Fanny dismissively. "Didn't I say you are like the daughter I never had? Besides I am enjoying it all enormously myself. It's the least I can do for the daughter of the Bejewelled One. Sleep well child."

With that she swept out of the room.

Leonie sat up with a start. What did Lady Fanny mean by calling mama the Bejewelled One? Was that her name? Did it have anything to do with the jewels that Mickey wanted her to steal? With all these thoughts, she tossed and turned the night away.

Adrian too was plagued by a strange restlessness that night. He gave up on sleep and went to down to his study to open the safe. From inside there, he rummaged through the jewel cases and slowly picked one out. He brought it out and sat it on his desk and slowly removed the lid. There sparkling in the candlelight sat an emerald as big as a goose's egg.

"Now, why have you become so important my beauty that half the world is trying to steal you?" he mused aloud. There is a mystery here that needs solving. He replaced the jewel back in its case and placed it in the safe and locked it.

CHAPTER NINE

Restless though her sleep was by the time Leonie woke the next day, it was noon and by the time she had her breakfast in bed and finished her dressing, it was early afternoon.

She stood shocked and entranced in the hallway as every available space was filled with bouquets. Roses of every shade, tulips imported from Holland, irises, lilies, they filled the hall, spilled out onto the foyer and right into the drawing rooms.

"Oh my goodness!" she exclaimed holding her hand to her chest.

"There you are dear child," said Lady Fanny stepping out of the breakfast parlour. "You are a success. See the number of bouquets that have been arriving nonstop since this morning," she said proudly as she made a sweeping gesture at the bouquets.

"So many my lady?" asked Leonie fascinated and a little afraid.

"Too little child," replied Lady Fanny tartly.

"So many would be when the bouquets start filling up our private chambers as well."

Then she laughed gaily and linked her hands with Leonie and strolled towards the drawing room.

"Come, let's comport ourselves for our callers will soon arrive," said Lady Fanny as she gave instructions to the butler to bring in the tea and cakes and admit their callers.

Soon the drawing room was tightly packed like a tin of sardines. His Grace arriving betimes found himself in the midst of a group of young gentlemen callers all surrounding Leonie reading poems to her eyes. Good lord!

Leonie lifted up her eyes at that moment and twinkled enchantingly at him. His mother commanded his attention and he went to obediently listen to her and the group of men around her when he heard Earl Billington offer Leonie a tool around the Park.

Leonie looked towards Lady Fanny who said instantly, "Make sure you take your parasol with you child."

Leonie nodded and went to get her wrap and bonnet and a matching parasol.

Adrian casually strolled over and stepped out in the hall and gently closed the door behind him and stood there waiting for her to appear.

In a while he heard voices from above stairs.

Leonie was talking to one of the maids, 'Polly, but think how much faster you can get your work done? There is nothing to it at all. It's polished to perfection. Here, let me show you."

As Adrian looked up, Leonie jumped onto the bannister and just when he made to stop her, she launched herself down. He stood at the right place where he knew she would land having slid down this particular bannister countless times himself. Smiling slightly, he watched her slide down laughing.

She saw him just when she neared the end and she forgot to jump and sailed right through into his arms. He caught her flush against him, a bundle of perfumed silk in his arms.

She was breathing hard, eyes sparkling, "Hello," she whispered.

He bent his head, "Hello imp," and their lips met. The fire within them ignited, glowed and sent flames through them. He reached down and cupped her bottom bringing her closer between his legs even as he bent her back to kiss her voraciously. He sucked deep of her mouth like a thirsty man and she shyly pandered to his needs. Her tongue flicked at his, taunted and teased him.

His hand feasted on her body, caressing, kneading. He slowed the kiss down and softly and gently lifted his head from hers. She looked up at him dazed. Her fingers went from clutching at his shoulders to touching her lips in awe and wonder.

"Come with me," he said urgently, setting her back on her feet.

She nodded and picked her wrap and bonnet and parasol from the floor that was dropped from her nerveless fingers during the kiss. He flung her into his coach and instructed to be driven to his house.

He looked at her seated across him clutching at her ridiculous silk wrap and said, "I have something to show you. This jewel that Mickey wanted you to steal."

She started on hearing the word Mickey and slowly nodded.

"Mickey won't bother you anymore," he said evenly.

She nodded. "Why is this jewel so important?"

"I was hoping you could tell me."

She shook her head. "I don't know your Grace. I only know he talked a lot about jewels. He didn't mention any particular one."

"Adrian," he said softly.

Leonie blushed and shook her head.

"Seeing as I have just kissed you and nearly ravished you in my mother's house, I think you are entitled to call me Adrian."

Her blush deepened and she wouldn't meet his eyes.

They arrived at his residence and soon she was seated in his study as he opened the safe and pulled out the jewel case. He took the emerald out and placed it on his desk and beckoned her, "Come closer, see the jewel."

She leaned across the desk and saw the jewel till she was cross-eyed. She lifted her eyes to find him close watching her watch the jewel.

"Your eyes are beautiful Adrian," she said dreamily and sighed. "Like this emerald, sparkling with fire and ice."

He laughed and a faint blush spread across his face.

She sat up excitedly and clapped her hands, "You are blushing, your Lordship."

"Minx! I should have beaten you when I had the chance," he said severely but his eyes twinkled.

She peeked enchantingly at him from beneath her eyelashes and said pertly, "I would like to try everything once, your Grace."

He laughed "Incorrigible chit."

She laughed as she stood up to walk around his desk and sat on his lap and wound her arms around his neck.

"Would you kiss me again Adrian? I do so like it when you kiss me."

"Good god Leonie," said Adrian sliding his hands around her waist and holding her firmly. "You will drive me mad, you know."

She smiled at him brilliantly and he bent his head and took her lips. She was aware of his hand gliding over her waist, stroking her back gently as he pulled her in closer.

Her body was on fire, she trembled with passion. She was in another world when she was locked in Adrian's arms. It was a world she secretly longed to return ever since the first time Adrian had kissed her. The hours she had spent reliving the kiss in her imagination now paled into insignificance as reality took its place.

He pulled at her sleeve and gently slid her bodice down freeing her breasts. He cupped one thumbing her nipple into arousal as she moaned loudly.

"Do you like that, my reckless little hoyden?" he asked huskily as he began to suck on her breast.

"Yes," she breathed. "I want you to kiss me and go on kissing me forever. I vow it is the most fascinating experience, your Grace."

"I am glad you find it so."

He licked her nipple and groaned, "My god, like the sweetest of berries."

Leonie moaned.

He pulled her skirts up and found the slit in her drawers and slid a finger in.

"Adrian," she gasped.

"Hush my love." He laughed and moistened his fingers with her juices. "Beautiful my sweet, already wet for me."

She blushed on hearing aloud about the dampness between her thighs and hid her head on his neck.

He kissed and nibbled at her throat as he began to circle her clit with his thumb.

"Oh Adrian!"

"Sweetheart, you must have a care." He laughed and groaned.

He slid his finger in and out arousing her to a peak that soon all her senses exploded in a starburst of pleasure and she tumbled headlong into bliss.

He looked at her in wonder, as she slowly opened her eyes and smiled shyly at him. He pulled his finger out of her and she blushed when she saw him lick his finger.

"Ah sweet love, you taste delicious."

She gave a cry and hid her face in his chest.

He laughed and dropped a kiss atop her curls. "But I am a brute for teasing you so, come I beg your pardon love."

"Adrian," she called shyly.

"Yes *mignonne*?"

"Can I stay here?"

His Grace was silent for a moment and then he lifted her and placed her on her feet.

"Child, one day you will meet a younger man than I who will make you happy."

Two great tears welled up in Leonie's eyes and she looked piteously at the Duke. "But I don't want a younger man."

"Child, I am no proper man for you."

"Your Grace, I never thought you would marry me," she said simply. "But I thought if you would like, you would take me. I would rather be yours than sold at the brothel."

There was a moment's silence and his Grace spoke so harshly that Leonie was startled.

"You are not to talk in such a fashion Leonie. Understand?"

"I am sorry, your Grace," she faltered.

"This is not how I think of you child."

"You don't love me," she nodded sadly. "You love Lady Marling."

His Grace took her hands and said, "I have never loved Lady Marling *mignonne.* What I thought was love pales in comparison to what I feel for you. I am no hero child. The years that separate us were ill-spent by me. I would give you a boy who would come to you with a clean heart."

One large tear glistened on the end of her lashes. "You need not have told me this your Grace. I know. I have always known for I have lived in St. Giles and I have seen much but I still love you."

His Grace looked deeply into her eyes and then went down on one knee and raised her hand to his lips, "*Ma belle,* since you will wed me, I pledge you my word that you shall never have cause to regret it."

Leonie flung herself at him and he opened his arms wide to receive her. They kissed deeply.

CHAPTER TEN

His Grace bundled her back into his carriage as soon as a maid set her to rights and helped refresh her. Now, he lounged across Leonie on the opposite side of the coach.

Dusk had arrived already and the street lamps flared here and there.

Leonie suddenly looked at him and said, "Adrian, my lady Fanny referred to my mother as the Bejewelled One. Think you that means anything?"

Adrian glanced at her with hooded eyes and said, "Let's ask her, shall we?"

Leonie nodded and fell silent and noted they had arrived.

The butler admitted them and informed his Grace that Lady Fanny was to be found in the morning room and if it pleases his Grace a moment alone for a word in private. His Grace looked in surprise at the butler and then gestured to Leonie to proceed.

"What is it?" his Grace asked.

"Your Grace, it was brought to my attention

that there is a man found watching the house at different times. I myself noticed him once."

"Really?"

"Yes your Grace. I have instructed the staff not to go out unnecessarily and on no account to converse with strangers."

"Excellent. I will look into it. I will be staying for dinner tonight."

"Yes, your Grace."

His Grace then strode into the morning room where he found his mother and his fiancée cosying up to each other. He smiled and said, "*Maman*, it pleases me to tell you that Leonie has accepted my offer of marriage."

Lady Fanny clapped in joy, "Oh dears. What wonderful news. You sly puss, you didn't mention this at all."

Leonie blushed and looked helplessly at Adrian.

He smiled and sat down in a chair by the window.

"I will start the wedding preparations immediately. You shall get married at St.George's…"

"No. I would prefer to get married at the Chateau," said Adrian firmly.

"But Adrian…" protested Lady Fanny.

"*Maman*, a quiet wedding with just a few friends and family is what we need at the moment."

Lady Fanny subsided muttering.

Adrian stiffened suddenly. He could sense a presence. He ever so slightly turned his head and there out of the corner of his eye, he could see a man standing on the street looking at the house.

"*Maman,* what do you know about the Bejewelled One?" he asked abruptly.

"That's how Leonie's mother, the Duchess of Andover was known as; for her name translated in the Hindoo language meant the Bejewelled One. That's how the Duke used to call her, my jewel, he used to say." Lady Fanny fondly recalled.

Leonie found herself all teary-eyed.

"There, there child," said Lady Fanny patting her.

"I don't remember much my lady. But I want to. I so want to," said Leonie.

"I understand child," said Lady Fanny hugging her.

Adrian stood up and silently stepped out of the room. He walked to the library and peeked through the curtains to find the man had dropped into the garden and even now was making his way swiftly to the house. Adrian waited to see where he would go. The man made for the study and stood there peering into it.

Adrian climbed out of the window and crept up onto him. His sword drew a drop of blood pointed as it was at his neck. "What do you want?"

The man turned slowly with his hands held high. Adrian looked at him in surprise. This was no man from the rookeries.

"You have something of mine," said the man.

"The jewel?" asked Adrian still holding the sword.

"Something more precious than the jewel."

"Leonie?"

The man nodded briefly.

"Dominic?" Adrian cocked an eyebrow.

The man looked in surprise and faint shock.

Adrian removed his sword and said, "Come, we have much to talk."

He took him directly into the morning room where Lady Fanny gave a start on seeing him.

"Adrian! Whatever are you up to? Popping in and out like a jack in the box," she complained and then turned to examine the man standing still next to Adrian. "Who do we have here?"

"An answer to a puzzle," said Adrian as he walked forward and rang the bell.

When the butler answered the summons, he said, "Inform Anna that her presence is required immediately in the morning room."

The butler bowed and withdrew.

"Adrian, now you are being mysterious," protested Lady Fanny.

"If I am not mistaken, this here is Dominic,

the Duke of Andover," said Adrian.

Both the ladies gasped in astonishment.

"Andover? The missing heir?"

"Dominic? My big brother?"

"The mystery will be solved when Anna identifies him correctly," said Adrian.

On cue, Anna opened the door and stepped into the room and gave a start on looking at Dominic.

"Oh my god! Your Grace!" she screamed and ran to Dominic and dropped into a curtsy. "Oh I prayed that you were safe and sound, your Grace."

"Rise Anna! I thank you for looking after my little sister so well," said Dominic gravely.

"I didn't do a very good job, your Grace," said Anna and burst into tears.

"Oh Anna! That's not true," cried Leonie running to Anna and hugging her. "She worked very hard to protect me and provide for me. I will not let anyone criticise her."

She said and turned mutinously towards Dominic challenging him to criticise her.

Dominic laughed and held open his arms, "Won't you give me a hug little sister? I haven't seen you since forever."

"Oh Dominic!"cried Leonie and hugged him. "I heard so much about you from Anna, and I missed you so. You are my big brother always playing pranks in the nursery."

Dominic looked at Anna reproachfully, "Ah Anna, did you have to tell her all that?"

"'Tis the truth your Grace," Anna sniffed.

"I missed your growing up years little sister but you have grown up to be such a fine young lady," said Dominic dropping a kiss atop her curls.

"Oh and Dominic, this here is the Dowager Duchess Lady Fanny Winterbourne and this is the Duke of Winterbourne, Adrian and my fiancé," she finished shyly.

Dominic cocked an eyebrow at Adrian and Adrian shrugged his shoulders and inclined his head.

"Come child, sit yourself down and your brother," said Lady Fanny. "Anna, be a dear and ring for some tea."

"I, for one, need a drink," said Adrian.

When the butler arrived he duly noted tea for the ladies and wine for the gentlemen.

"Where have you been all this time Leonie and what have you been doing?" Dominic asked dropping into a chair next to the sofa.

"Your Grace," said Anna apologetically, "When you told us all to run and hide, I thought London would be the perfect place and right sorry I am to have brought Lady Leonie here. The troubles she went through."

"That's not true Anna," protested Leonie.

"Anna needed to work to take care of me and it is easier to find a job in London than in the countryside isn't it? And she worked tirelessly to take care of me, Dominic."

"I will not criticise you Anna," said Dominic quietly. "You have done the best in a very bad situation. For which I am very grateful."

Leonie beamed with affection and Anna looked relieved.

Adrian sipping his drink said, "What I would like to know is why Leonie is being harassed for a jewel?"

Anna gasped in horror and cast a fearful glance at Dominic.

Dominic sighed and said, "The story goes that papa helped mama escape from a neighbouring king and he brought her to England with him. Her father gifted her with what is known as the Queen's Jewels. They are fabled and worth more than a king's ransom. Mama bequeathed the jewels to us children. So each one of us have our own jewel."

"But I don't have any jewels," said Leonie confused.

Dominic looked at Anna who said tearfully, "Milady, you were given a jewel by your mama. When we were asked to escape, the jewel was entrusted in my care. When we first arrived in London, someone stole the jewel from me. I am so sorry."

Leonie reached out and patted Anna sympathetically, "Its' okay Anna. Don't worry."

"That is true," said Lady Fanny hearing the story with rapt attention. "I was there that night at the party when your dear mother proclaimed Dominic as the heir to the dukedom and then handed out to each of her children one precious jewel."

Dominic nodded in agreement and said, "Leonie's jewel was an emerald."

Leonie gasped out loud and her eyes flew to Adrian who frowned at the information.

"Adrian, was that...do you think?"

Adrian said thoughtfully, "It is true that I am in possession of an emerald which Leonie was trying to steal when I first met her."

Leonie gasped and hid her face in her hands.

"Mickey made me do it, so I can free Anna from prison."

"Although, she didn't have a clue what to steal," said Adrian amused.

"Well, I like that. I am not a thief!" said Leonie indignantly.

"Mickey was unusually persistent in trying to steal the emerald and when asked he told me he was being hounded by some people from India for the jewel or the girl."

"Was?" asked Dominic staring strangely at Adrian.

Adrian nodded briefly, "Was. I believe he

understood the perils of accosting a member of my family."

Dominic nodded in agreement.

The ladies witnessed this strange conversation and were confused.

Leonie suddenly asked, "How did you find me Dominic?"

"I was informed Anna was imprisoned falsely. But when I went to get her released, I was told that she was already free and taken away by the Duke of Winterbourne. Then as I was being pursued by the Rajah's men, it behoved upon me to turn the tables on them. So as I was watching them, I learnt they had sent Mickey to steal a jewel. I traced Mickey to a tavern called Hammer and Tongs…

Adrian stiffened a little and exchanged a quick glance with Dominic.

Dominic continued "But I missed him by a few minutes. So the only other clue I had was the Duke of Winterbourne. So I went to your house and then followed you here and came to know that your mother had a new ward that she was launching in Society by the name, Leonie. I waited to talk to Anna or Leonie but neither would step outside the house or be alone at any time. Today, I thought I will get into the house and see for myself. And here I am."

"Oh my goodness! What a tale! My head is spinning already," said Lady Fanny.

"I suggest you ladies retire and get some rest.

And we can all meet at dinner," Adrian suggested.

The ladies nodded and retired gracefully from the room leaving the gentlemen staring at each other.

CHAPTER ELEVEN

"I can introduce you to the Ton if you please, Andover," offered Adrian looking hard at the tall, silent man standing in front of him holding a thousand storms inside of him.

"Dominic please," he offered and then shook his head. "I still have the rest of my brothers and sisters to find and I would rather no harm come to them."

"You don't think announcing yourself as the Duke of Andover would bring them out from their hiding?" asked Adrian.

"I would not claim the dukedom until all my brothers and sisters are safe," said Dominic firmly.

Adrian sighed. "I will not pretend to understand but I will support you seeing as I am marrying your sister."

Dominic looked up in surprise.

Adrian lazily held up a hand and said coldly, "Before you tell me I am too old for her. I have to tell you, really, I find I don't much care what you think.

She will be my wife with or without your blessing."

"I was only going to offer you my congratulations," said Dominic mildly. "Although seeing as how well you have taken care of her so as to not to let a whiff of scandal besmirch her good name, I can only be grateful."

Adrian made a dismissive wave at that but a faint tinge of colour touched his cheeks.

"How many brothers and sisters do you have?" Adrian asked curiously.

"I am the eldest of ten," said Dominic shortly. "But thus far, I have been able to trace the whereabouts of only three including Leonie."

"Really? Pray tell, where they are, Leonie would be pleased to have them attend the wedding. I was planning a quiet affair at my estate, Chateau de Winter."

"Her eldest sister, Sita, was born next to me, and is married to Julian, the Earl of Stonebridge and is known as his Aunt Clara's niece. Next to Sita was born, Leila, who is married to Richard, the Marquess of Rivenhall and is quietly settled at their estate in Cumbria. And now, I have found Leonie, whom your mother claims as her ward."

"What are you going to do next?" asked Adrian.

Dominic threw a speculative glance at Adrian and moved restlessly to the window. "They will find me soon enough. I can't stay in one place for long. Thus far, I have impressed upon my two sisters to lay low and their husbands, I find, are quite capable of protecting them."

Adrian poured out some brandy from the sideboard and handing Dominic a glass said, "My instincts tell me that you have to take this game to them Dominic. Usually, they are seeking you. It's time to turn the tables and seek them out."

"And then what?" asked Dominic sipping the fine brandy.

Adrian shrugged, "Unpleasant though it may be, but we both know they are not uncommon. We merely eliminate them by such means."

"I am not certain if it would help. If not one group of men, it will be another. And these men are known to buy thugs from the dockside."

"Either their spies are good or they are merely keeping an eye on you and are trying to stay one step ahead of you."

Dominic thought for a moment and said, "Perhaps, I shall ask your help in this investigation."

Adrian nodded, gazing out of the window into the dark gardens lit here and there with fairy lamps, his mother's idea no doubt. A little bit of whimsicality.

"Very well, it will be like old times. It might even be successful, who knows."

He slid Dominic a sharp glance. "I will, naturally, expect you to remain discrete in this matter.

My fiancée and my mother must not know of this little jaunt of ours."

Dominic assumed an expression of insulted innocence, "Discretion is the only virtue I have left," he said sadly.

The butler knocked and opened the door and announced, "Dinner is served your Grace."

Both the gentlemen walked out of the room to find the ladies coming down the stairs to them and together they made their way to the dining room.

The long room was lit by candles that stood in gold clusters on the table. Silver shined and crystal glass winked and a mellow light bathed it all.

At the head of the table sat his Grace, the Duke of Winterbourne with the Dowager duchess, Lady Fanny Winterbourne on his right and his fiancée, Lady Leonie Andover on his left. Opposite to him at the foot of the table sat his Grace, Duke of Andover.

Course after course was brought in and discretely served.

"What is this child? A very pretty dagger," commented Lady Fanny as Leonie had a dagger tucked into the ribbon at her waist.

Leonie blushed and said, "It was a gift from his Grace, my lady. Anna said mama was an expert in daggers and when I asked, his Grace taught me how to throw a dagger."

"Oh my goodness!" exclaimed Lady Fanny.

"Whatever will you be at next?"

"It is true, mama was an expert at swords and daggers," nodded Dominic.

"You are not to encourage her Adrian," said Lady Fanny. "I vow it is scandalous."

Leonie twinkled merrily. "There is one other thing I made his Grace teach me that is very bloodthirsty."

"What is it child?"

"I will not tell," she shook her head wisely. "You will say it's unladylike."

"Oh Adrian, what have you been at? Some hoydenish trick I dare say."

"What is it? Do tell, you have whetted our curiosity now," asked Dominic.

"No, no!" Leonie pursued her mouth primly. "His Grace is not to tell."

"One would infer it to be some disgraceful secret, minx," said his Grace smiling fondly at her.

"Well, my lady would think so," said Leonie doubtfully looking at her future mother-in-law.

Lady Fanny laughed and said, "Oh go on child, what is it?"

"I only learnt how to fence, my lady," said Leonie excitedly.

"Oh la! Whatever will you think of next!" exclaimed Lady Fanny. "What a child she is! I vow I would never have dared speak thus at her age."

There was a shout of laughter and Winterbourne's eyes were alight with it. He flicked his finger across Leonie's cheek. She chuckled and turned jubilantly at the others.

"Oh, it's good to have a family!"

Dominic smiled indulgently although his eyes darkened for a moment in sadness.

"I hope to be able to introduce your two elder sisters to you shortly Leonie."

Leonie looked up shocked. "You have found my sisters? Sita and Leila? Anna used to tell me about them."

Dominic nodded. "Sita is now married to the Earl of Stonebridge, while Leila is married to the Marquess of Rivenhall."

Lady Fanny nodded intently. "They are good families. I have known Clara forever. We both made our debuts together, you know."

"Oh, can we invite them for our wedding, your Grace?" asked Leonie.

"Of course, my dear. We will send out the invitations soon."

After dinner, the ladies decided to forgo the ritual of leaving the gentlemen to their port and they all sat in the drawing room, the ladies sipping their tea, while the gentlemen indulged in a little brandy.

They discussed the upcoming wedding and whom to invite and finally decided to keep it only to their immediate family and perhaps the tenants of de Winter estate who would greatly look forward to the news of their Duke's wedding.

"We should send ahead our luggage and the invitations tomorrow and we will start two days hence. That ought to give you ample time to order your dresses *maman* and also give time for the others to travel for the wedding."

"That's hardly any time at all Adrian but we will see what we can manage," sniffed Lady Fanny.

"Come child," she said and stood up fluffing her skirts. "If the luggage has to leave tomorrow we better start the packing now. Let's leave the gentlemen for the evening."

The gentlemen stood up and bowed. Leonie curtsied prettily and went out of the room after Lady Fanny.

Adrian glanced at Dominic and said, "Shall we begin the hunt tonight?"

Dominic nodded and said, "Nothing like the moment. But you cannot be going into the stews dressed like that. Although from what I heard, last time you were dressed even more exotically."

"Last time, I saw Leonie safe in her bedchamber when she should have been dancing the night away at her first ball merely because she took a step in Lady Hamilton's gardens and Mickey accosted her. Luckily I arrived on time, she could hardly return to the ball in a torn gown and so I brought her here. I didn't think it necessary to change my clothes for a gutter rat."

Dominic's eyes glowed with anger, "Is that why you slit his throat?"

Adrian nodded grimly. "And left a message. Nobody toys with mine."

"I should have been the one to do that," said Dominic angrily.

"Give way. I was there before you," said Adrian simply. "Now if you would cool your heels and your anger awhile, I will change and be with you in a moment."

Dominic nodded. Adrian strode out of the room.

CHAPTER TWELVE

Later that night, Adrian accompanied by Dominic stepped down from the hackney into the very heart of one of London's dirtiest and dangerous stews. It had started raining an hour ago and the paving stones underfoot became slick with rain and refuse. Moonlight tried its hardest to soften the grime and squalor but to no avail. It merely threw it all in high relief.

"You know what, Dominic, it concerns me somewhat that you know your way so well around this part of Town."

Adrian saw a pair of beady eyes glinting in the shadows and casually he used his ebony walking stick to discourage the rat which was the size of a slinking human. The creature vanished into the vast network of alleyways.

Dominic chuckled softly, "Be grateful that I know my way around since I will know my way out as well."

"You will have to learn to refrain from amusing yourself in places such as this when you acknowledge your dukedom. I cannot see your family approving this sort of outing."

"True but I trust once I have my family together I expect to have far more interesting things to do in the evenings than dive in the stews."

Dominic paused to get his bearings. "There is the lane we want. The man we are seeking has arranged to meet us in the tavern at the end of this filthy street."

"Your information is correct and can be trusted?"

Dominic shrugged. "No but it is a starting point. He was paid to abduct Leonie apparently when the steal went awry but Leonie being so closely guarded, he didn't receive his money and now he is disgruntled for he didn't get paid for his troubles of stalking her."

Adrian tightened his grip on his walking stick. "Stalking?" he asked calmly.

"We shall no doubt discover the truth soon enough."

The lights of the dinghy tavern shone a dull yellow glow through the small windows which were covered in filth. Adrian and Dominic pushed their way inside and found the interior stinking of foul ale and smoky due to the fire in the hearth.

There was a rabid atmosphere about the place like its people were just waiting for a fight to break out. The patrons were packed shoulder to shoulder along the long wooden trestle tables and several of them glanced up as they made their way in.

Each pair of greedy eyes noted the shabbiness of the coat and the worn boots both Adrian and Dominic donned for the occasion. Adrian could almost hear the collective sigh of regret as the patrons decided they weren't worthy prey.

"There's our man" said Dominic leading the way to the side of the tavern. Near the window, I was told he would be wearing a checker scarf and cap.

The thug had small beady eyes drowned in ale which darted about constantly never staying focused on anything in particular. He was wearing the regulation scarf and cap Adrian thought as they strode over to his table.

The thug opened his mouth to speak and Adrian saw two rotting teeth and a gaping hole of a mouth.

"You be the coves what wants to know about the brown man?"

"You have the right of it," Dominic said sliding down the wooden bench across from the thug.

He was aware that Adrian stood, his gaze moving with deceptive calm as he casually quartered the taproom and monitored the patrons.

"What can you tell us about him?"

"It will cost ye," the thug grinned.

"Payment only when the information is good."

The thug leaned forward and said with a conspiratorial air. "I was busting my bum by the dockside warehouses and in my break, the brown man and another white chappie walked over to me and asked how would I like to make some easy money."

He cackled with laughter and downed the ale and threw the tankard.

"As if I would say no. So I asked him what's his lay, and he tells me as to how this gel is from the stews but is setting herself up as a nabob's daughter and that she should be brought down a peg or two. So I stalked her a day or two but she was locked up tight alright."

Dominic sensed Adrian stiffened ever so slightly.

"Where do I find the brown man and the white?" Adrian asked casually flipping a coin.

The thug, his poisonous breath wafting across the table, said "They be finding you."

"Convenient," murmured Adrian.

Dominic sat silent for a moment and then he slowly got to his feet. "Let us be off brother," he murmured to Adrian. "We have wasted our time this night."

The thug scowled in alarm, "Ere now, what about me blunt?"

Adrian tossed the coin he had been flipping

about and just as the thug reached up to catch it, Adrian caught him by the back of his head and slammed his face onto the wooden table. The satisfying crunch of bones breaking could be heard.

The thug squealed like a pig and Dominic aware that that there was a stir of interest amongst the tavern patrons as they turned to see what the commotion was all about.

"The back door I think," Dominic said to Adrian.

"Excellent. After you," said Adrian suddenly holding a dagger in his hand as he clutched the thug's hair and tugged him backwards until his neck was exposed.

"This is so you never stalk a girl again!" And he slit his throat and left him bleeding to death.

Cleaning his dagger on the thug's jacket, he turned and left by the back door. Dominic right behind him, slamming the door shut on the angry shouts of the tavern keeper and his restless horde of patrons.

"Well, well, well, what do we have here?" asked Adrian as he came to a stop when a brown man and a white man stepped out from the shadows.

Moonlight gleaming on the knives they held they leapt for the throats.

Adrian twisted the gold top of his walking stick and out came a sword which he swung in a slashing arc. The sword struck his assailant's hand and the knife bounded harmlessly onto the ground. And he twisted and pressed the sword point against the assailant's neck.

He skewered him in a moment and turned to see Dominic do the same to the other man.

"Best be on our way," said Dominic cheerfully with only a passing glance at Adrian's victim. "I expect the rowdy patrons will be spilling out of the door in a minute."

"I have no intention of delaying our departure," Adrian slid his sword inside the ebony stick and twisted the top as the blade disappeared as silently as it appeared.

Dominic led the way and Adrian followed. They raced out of the lane where Dominic unhesitatingly turned left. Thanks to his intimate knowledge of the underbelly of the city, they soon found themselves standing in a corner of a relatively safe street.

Adrian used his walking stick to hail a hackney which arrived soon. He bounded up into the hackney closely followed by Dominic who dropped into the seat across from Adrian.

A thoughtful silence prevailed within as Adrian idly pursued the dark streets out of the window and Dominic watched him from the shadows. Soon a laugh began to burst out of Dominic.

Adrian turned in surprise.

"That was interesting was it not?" asked Dominic laughing. "Do you go about decimating your fellow people?"

"Yes, if they are a threat to Leonie."

"What do you make of it?"

Adrian went over the events of the evening and concluded, "You were setup. They weren't expecting you to bring along a friend. They thought you would be alone and they could very well have killed you."

Dominic's laughter stopped. "But they didn't."

"No, they didn't.

"I have never before been able to kill the Rajah's men in England. They always work behind the scenes and when we do meet face-to-face, they escape at the most opportune moment."

"So you have killed the Rajah's men not-in-England?"

Dominic looked at Adrian and slowly closed his eyes.

"How many of them are running around in this part of the world?"

"I don't know. I have only ever seen this one."

"Well, let's consider that we have eliminated one of the Rajah's men and presume that there was only one. So looks like you have earned a few months of reprieve."

"That's certainly one way of looking at it."

"Well, do so. Now is a good time to spend with the family you have. Come to Chateau de Winter for the wedding and spend time with your sisters there. You all need to heal. Sure I have provided Leonie wealth and some measure of happiness but you need to understand that she lives in fear. Fear that her parents were taken from her. Fear that her family was taken from her. Fear that her childhood was stolen from her. Fear that Anna will be taken from her. Fear that I might leave her. Fear is the only world she knows. Don't mistake her *joie d vivre;* it is a tool she uses to cover up for her fear."

"You have studied her well," said Dominic quietly.

"I love her," Adrian said simply and fell silent.

CHAPTER THIRTEEN

By the time they arrived at Chateau de Winter, it was dusk. Leonie was sitting with her face plastered to the window of the Winterbourne traveling carriage talking animatedly to her brother and describing the glories of Chateau de Winter, while his Grace looked on indulgently and Lady Fanny with amusement.

When she spotted the hulking outline of an old castle looming up out of the mist, she cried out, "Here Dominic, I told you it looks like a fairy castle."

In the odd evening light, it looked like an illusion that might disappear if she so much as blinked; an enchanted castle springing up out of a fairy tale.

Dominic straightened with sudden interest, "Good heavens, Adrian, what is that?"

"That is Chateau de Winter."

"Your home?" he turned to him. "You live in a castle?"

His Grace's mouth curved faintly in a smile,

"Leonie adores it."

Leonie nodded her in agreement. "Isn't it wonderful Dominic? Imagine living in such a marvelous place. I think it suits Adrian."

"It suits you too, my love."

"Yes," she agreed utterly enthralled. "I have always dreamt of living in a castle."

When the carriage rolled to a stop in front of the Chateau, his Grace descended first and turned in time to catch Leonie, who simply jumped out of the carriage straight into his arms and slowly slid down all six feet seven inches of him to the ground.

His eyes darkened with passion as he dropped a kiss atop her chocolate curls and said, "Minx!"

Leonie threw him a saucy smile and stepped into the Great Hall. They were promptly followed by Lady Fanny and Dominic.

The butler informed them that the Earl and Countess of Stonebridge had already arrived and were refreshing themselves in time for dinner. And the Marquess and the Marchioness of Rivenhall would arrive in time for dinner.

"Excellent! Show the ladies to their chambers Gibbons."

Turning to Dominic, he said, "Come, I will show you to your rooms."

Leonie was bubbling with enthusiasm. She had her sisters and brother with her for her wedding and she was getting married to Adrian and she was going to live in a castle.

Later when they sat down to dinner, she expressed her wish to show the castle to her sisters and brother.

"I love Chateau de Winter, Sita," Leonie explained as the butler poured wine into her glass.

"I cannot wait for you all to see it in the morning."

She looked at Adrian expectantly.

"I shall take you on a tour soon," his Grace promised.

A fierce anticipation gripped Adrian as he gazed upon her. Leonie's gentle soft rounded shoulders and the upper swells of her breasts were as pale as moonlight in the glow of candles. The dark highlights of her chocolate hair gleamed. Her caramel eyes were brilliant and mysterious. He could see the slight blush that tinged her cheeks and knew she was thinking about him.

He had a sudden fierce urge to pick her up in his arms and carry her straight upstairs to his bed. Soon, he promised himself. Very soon she would be completely his.

"I owe Leonie, looking at you so beautiful and poised I can hardly remember the little imp you were as a child," Sita was telling.

Leonie laughed. "You must ask Anna, I was still very much an imp growing up."

"She still is," said his Grace smiling.

Leonie flashed her eyes, "I am not. I am a lady."

They all laughed at that.

"I remember you Sita as always taking care of us. Even in the nursery, we would heed you. I think you were always keeping us in order."

"She is still taking care of us," said Julian gazing fondly at his wife.

"Don't believe a word these two are telling, your Grace," Sita protested looking at Adrian. "I too was quite a hoyden."

"That would be me," interjected Leila smoothly. "Sita was the peacemaker."

"I am so glad to see you all carry daggers," exclaimed Leonie when she noticed that her sisters like her had daggers tucked into their waistbands.

Sita and Leila exchanged glances and said together, "That was mama's idea."

"She would always carry a couple of daggers on her person," said Sita.

"And papa would protest saying he never knew who needed protection more, him or her," said Leila laughing.

The dinner was a splendid affair and Dominic was glad he let himself be persuaded by Adrian to spend time with his sisters at the Chateau. There was so much of the in-between years that shaped them and made them grow into different people that he didn't know about and he wanted to know all of it.

Soon they retired for the night as Lady Fanny recommended. "You don't want to have dark circles under your eyes on your wedding day child."

Leonie nodded and she and her sisters giggled all the way up to their chambers where they hugged and kissed each other goodbye.

Leonie curled up on the sofa right in front of the fireplace. She wore only a thin robe and nothing else. The warmth of the flames felt good. She liked the way the flames licked and leapt and danced on the wall.

But she was nervous. She pretended to be normal the entire dinner and it was such a strain.

Her elder sisters were beautiful, self-possessed ladies and she felt like a gutter rat imitating a princess. She was waiting for Adrian to come upstairs to his bedchamber which she was told was next to hers.

She was dozing off when she heard the door's soft snick and it silently swung open. She looked up sleepily and saw Adrian standing at the door in a maroon brocade dressing gown. Her mouth fell open. God! He was so handsome. What if she didn't deserve him?

"What is it *bebe*? Not asleep yet?" he asked closing the door and strolling inside.

Leonie stood up and his mouth went dry. He could see her completely nude with the firelight in the background. She looked like a pagan goddess with her chocolate hair unbound and flowing freely down her back. Her high round breasts with dark nipples. He looked down at her triangle of hair between her thighs. He looked up at her lush caramel eyes looking up at him with worry - worry?

"Are you nervous Leonie?" he asked softly coming to stand in front of her.

"I am not nervous." It was a blatant lie.

"What is it my love? What is troubling you?"

"Why don't we go someplace where we can be alone Adrian?" asked Leonie wrapping her arms around his waist and pressing up to him.

He immediately took her into his arms. "You have your sisters and brother with you. Aren't you happy?"

"I am but I feel like they are all strangers and they are talking about some other person who is not me."

"Ah my love," said Adrian and sat down on the sofa and pulled Leonie down on his lap. "Give it time. They have their memories and you have yours and in-between you all have had your independent growing up years. It might take years to catch up but suffice that the door has opened a little between you all. Cherish the moment, love and just enjoy it. You don't have to prove anything to anyone."

"When I am in your arms Adrian, it's the only time I feel safe and confident. I sometimes feel like I am playing at make-believe I used to play as a child," confided Leonie resting her head on his shoulder.

"When the wedding is over, you will feel that they are your family. You will know that we are family."

She smiled nervously, "Sometimes the dream is better than reality, isn't it?"

Adrian bent his head and kissed her. His mouth was hot and moist, his tongue dancing with hers suggestively. Her fingers slid deep into his thick luscious golden hair and then slid down his shoulders to his chest where she found an opening in the robe and she slid her hand inside.

Adrian sucked in his breath at the feel of her soft hand caressing his chest.

"You cannot wait a few hours?" he teased her. "I am trying my best to keep you a virgin until the wedding my love."

Her eyes darkened with passion and she slowly let her robe slip over her shoulders, "I want you, Adrian."

His body tightened painfully hard and throbbing in anticipation. She blew softly on his lips and slowly traced its contours with her pink tongue.

A rough groan escaped from his throat.

Leonie laughed softly. "I am not quite sure what you want, your Grace," she teased.

His fist bunched in her tousled hair. "I will make myself perfectly clear. Open your mouth."

She obediently opened her mouth and he ravished her mouth. Plundering its hidden depths and secret places and drinking deep from her mouth. He ruthlessly pulled her robe open revealing her body to his gaze. He licked and kissed her breasts sucking on them until she was mindless with passion.

His fingers slid down her taut stomach and down to her curls between her thighs where he cupped her and parted her secret garden lush with passion. He dipped a finger into her sheath, hot, moist and slick and so tight he was shuddering with pleasure at the thought of sinking himself deep into her.

It was her desire, her need that drove the pace now. And Adrian let her set the pace. He watched her skin glow in the firelight as she thrashed in his arms seeking her pleasure. He caught the back of her head and brought her face to his thrusting his tongue wildly into her mouth. She soared in his arms and exploded with pleasure.

He watched her slowly return to him, she fluttered her long eyelashes and opened them shyly. He very carefully lifted her up and carried her to her bed and placed her in the centre of it. He dropped a kiss on the curls between her thighs.

"Goodnight *mignonne,* dream of us," he whispered as he kissed her gently.

"Goodnight Adrian, I love you," she said and her eyelashes fluttered close.

The wedding was out of a fairy tale. Her dress was sheer Belgian antique lace and she looked like a fairy princess in it.

His Grace, the Duke of Andover, Dominic walked her down the aisle. The villagers were all happy to see their Lord Duke getting married. They had come dressed in their best clothes and showered flower petals on her as she walked towards the altar.

Her sisters were seated with their husbands in the front row as was her soon to be mother-in-law, Lady Fanny Winterbourne. Lady Clara Beddington was unable to attend the wedding for she had still not recovered enough for long travel. But she sent her best wishes to the happy couple.

But her eyes remain locked with Adrian's. He looked tall and handsome and impossibly courtly. He took her breath away and she blushed thinking of how wantonly she behaved last night.

But as she approached on Dominic's arm, she knew this was right. She loved him. With her eyes held captive by his smouldering emerald gaze, Leonie put her small hand in his large one without hesitation, fully prepared to make her vows.

After the exchange of vows, he placed an exquisite diamond ring on her finger. Then he lifted her veil and kissed his bride. And finally, he plucked from a silver tray a diamond studded tiara with the fabled Queen's jewel, an enormous emerald in the centre and placed it on her head, atop her chocolate curls.

He clasped her hand in his and turned towards

the guests and said, "Ladies and gentlemen, I have the honour to present to you all my Duchess, Leonie Winterbourne."

THE END

AFTERWORD

The idea for The Bejewelled Family Saga came upon me in 2015. But due to various personal commitments, I didn't really get around to start work on this series. I was content to merely work out the titles and the little poems that go with the Jewels and left it at that. It was only during the "Lockdown" that I turned to look at my unfinished work and was inspired to take up writing and completing the series. It was an outpouring of love and labour, a burst of excitement and creation, a waltz of characters dancing their way to tell their side of the story. This is the first story in this series that I began to write, so needless to say the hero and heroine are my favorite characters.

ABOUT THE AUTHOR

R. J. Kalpana

R. J. Kalpana is an Indian novelist, short story writer, a critic and a management consultant. She earned her PhD on Feminist Issues in Indian Literature. She is now branching into writing historical romance fiction.

THE BEJEWELLED FAMILY SAGA

The Bejewelled Family Saga is the story of love and loss of a family. We follow the family from the parents enchanting romance to the children's own coming of age challenges. It takes us from the palaces of India to the ducal estates of England, from the gutters of London to the high Ton of English Society. It is the story of an Indian Queen's fabled Jewels and the enemies that seek to covet it.

The Bejewelled One

It is a tale as old as time, of an enchanting romance between an Indian Queen and an English Duke. He helps her escape her enemies and takes her to the ducal estates in England. The Queen's fabled jewels are much coveted by the enemies who aren't afraid to kill on English soil.

Opals For Hope

Lady Sita is on the run and when she comes upon a Lady of the manor lying ill and unattended, she

decides to stay on and help until her nephew Lord Julian Stonebridge arrives from India and looks with suspicion upon his newest cousin. In midst of all this, trouble comes calling in the guise of the Rajah's men and her long-lost brother Dominic.

Amethysts For Love

Leila is London's most beautiful courtesan and legendary are the men at her pretty feet styled as she is as the Indian princess. Lord Richard Rivenhall is a spy in the Foreign Office and clues lead him to think that she is a traitor. Leila is not who Richard thinks she is but she has her own deadliest secrets to hide.

Emeralds For Envy

Coerced into being a jewel thief, Leonie breaks into the Devil Duke's mansion and is caught red-handed by the Devil himself. From the gutters of London she grew up innocent and as pristine as a lotus amongst pond slime and he was so disillusioned by human nature that nothing stirred his interest anymore. Would this reckless beauty bring him back from the edge of darkness before fate intrudes in the guise of her enemies?

Pearls For Innocence

Lord Spencer Huntingdon driven to purchase a commission to impress his fiancée returns from

the war a scarred cripple. Jilted, he now lives in the shadows of the Huntingdon Priory hiding his scarred face from the world warped in his aching loneliness and fear until one fateful night, a beautiful woman on the run stumbles upon him and warns him of jewel thieves. Lady Isha forced to dress up as a boy warns Lord Spencer and then stays on to cure him of a raging fever. But she doesn't stay long enough to find out if her herbs have healed his scars and his leg until they meet in the most exclusive ballroom of the Ton along with his ex-fiancee.

Sapphires For Danger

Davina becomes an unwilling witness to a race fixing racket and she rushes to inform the Marquis of Thorncourt that one of his men will soon betray him. Sylvester scorns her and so she disguises herself as a boy and trains his horses until Sylvester is forced to acknowledge the threat is real. They leave for London to discover more clues and there she meets her sister; now Duchess of Winterbourne. Davina knows Sylvester is the Ton's most eligible bachelor but will he offer her the love she desperately seeks?

Topaz For Fidelity

When wealthy heiress Lady Annbella Maybricks is importuned to marry by her odious uncle coveting her wealth, she takes matters in her own hands

and runs away and strikes a deal with a stranger at an inn. Lord Damian traveling incognito and on the run since his parents death looks upon her proposition with suspicion and then decides that marrying her and taking possession of her estate Greenwoods Park is the perfect disguise until his and her enemies catch up with them for a final reckoning.

Amber For Passion

Driven to get out of her stepbrother's clutches Helen Amberfeld took the opportunity when she was staked in a game of chance. She decided that she would rather walk away with Lucian who won her than remain with her stepbrother. But their journey to her estate was fraught with peril being chased by highwaymen and kidnappers until they finally arrive at Bellaview, her inheritance only to meet with Lucian's forbidding brother, Dominic who immediately suggested marriage. Was that her only option or would she be dragged by her step-brother and forced into marriage with his friend?

Diamonds For Tears

After spending years in the glittering ballrooms of the Ton, Miranda Mellors is bored to tears by the current crop of beau. Determined to marry a man of her choice she goes where no respectable lady should, into the most exclusive gaming hell of London where she discovers she is surrounded by the

rakes of the worst order only to be rescued by the mysterious owner of the famed gaming hell. Lord Wulfric had delayed his entry into Society awaiting his brother. They meet at the Duke of Winterbourne's Chateau d' Winter for a family reunion where they are followed by their enemies who boldly attack the ladies leaving Miranda bewildered and out-of-depth amidst this bold family.

Corals For Remembrance

Caught red-handed in the arms of a notorious fortune hunter and publicly denounced by her fiancé Lady Rosalyn Anderson at Lady Whistledon's ball, Lady Rosalyn is furious with her parents and the Ton and decides to run away. She boards the ship 'Coral Lady' and finds she had just handed her virginity to the captain. Will Tristan leave the memories of his dark past behind long enough for him to embrace the present or will the return of his brother Dominic into his life be the trigger that will loosen the demons within?

Rubies For Revenge

Lady Sybila Overton is forced into an engagement with the Rajah of Shamapur. Unable to go through the farce of a marriage she contemplates shooting herself when she is rescued by the Duke of Andover. The elusive Duke has come back from the dead to claim his dukedom and finally end the feud be-

tween himself and the Rajah - to take revenge for his parent's deaths. In a world where treachery and betrayal reign, a world where greed and lust rule, Lady Sybila is trapped in a desperate web of fears, murder and intrigue. Does she and Dominic have the courage to reach out to the destiny of love that all the forces of the world cannot defeat?

BOOKS BY THIS AUTHOR

The Bejewelled One

It is a tale as old as time, of an enchanting romance between an Indian Queen and an English Duke. He helps her escape her enemies and takes her to the ducal estates in England. The Queen's fabled jewels are much coveted by the enemies who aren't afraid to kill on English soil.

Opals For Hope

Lady Sita is on the run and when she comes upon a Lady of the manor lying ill and unattended, she decides to stay on and help until her nephew Lord Julian Stonebridge arrives from India and looks with suspicion upon his newest cousin. In midst of all this, trouble comes calling in the guise of the Rajah's men and her long-lost brother Dominic.

Amethysts For Love

Leila is London's most beautiful courtesan and legendary are the men at her pretty feet styled as she is as the Indian princess. Lord Richard Rivenhall is a spy in the Foreign Office and clues lead him to think that she is a traitor. Leila is not who Richard thinks she is but she has her own deadliest secrets to hide.

Printed in Great Britain
by Amazon